FRUITS

A Caribbean Counting Poem

For Tamara, Ashley and Jody, with love - V.B.
To Cherry and Sophie - D.A.

'Fruits' is taken from *Duppy Jamboree*, first published by Cambridge University Press in 1992
This edition published 2019 by Macmillan Children's Books
an imprint of Pan Macmillan
The Smithson, 6 Briset Street, London EC1M 5NR
EU representative: Macmillan Publishers Ireland Ltd, 1st Floor,
The Liffey Trust Centre, 117–126 Sheriff Street Upper,
Dublin 1, D01 YC43
Associated companies throughout the world
www.panmacmillan.com

ISBN: 978-1-5290-0756-5

Text copyright © Valerie Bloom 1992
Illustrations copyright © David Axtell 1997
Moral rights asserted.

The right of Valerie Bloom and David Axtell to be identified as the author and illustrator of this work
has been asserted by them in accordance with the Copyright, Designs and Patents Act 1988.

3 5 7 9 8 6 4 2

A CIP catalogue record for this book is available from the British Library.

Printed in China

FRUITS

A CARIBBEAN COUNTING POEM

by Valerie Bloom

Illustrated by David Axtell

MACMILLAN CHILDREN'S BOOKS

Half a pawpaw in the basket –

Only one o' we can have it.

Wonder which one that will be?

I have a feeling that is me.

One guinep up in the tree

Hanging down there tempting me.

It don' mek no sense to pick it,

One guinep can't feed a cricket.

Two ripe guava pon the shelf,

I know I hide them there meself.

When night come an' it get dark

Me an' them will have a talk.

Three sweet-sop, well I jus' might

Give one o' them a nice big bite.

Cover up the bite jus' so, sis,

Then no one will ever notice.

Four red apple near me chair –

Who so careless put them there?

Them don' know how me love apple?

Well, thank God fe silly people.

Five jew-plum, I can't believe it!

How they know jew-plum's me fav'rit?

But why they hide them in the cupboard?

Cho, people can be so awkward.

Six naseberry, you want a nibble?

Why baby must always dribble?

Come wipe you mout', it don't mek sense

To broadcast the evidence.

Seven mango! What a find!

The smaddy who lef them really kind.

One fe you an' six fe me,

If you want more, climb the tree.

Eight orange fe cousin Clem,

But I have just one problem –

How to get rid o' the eight skin

That the orange them come in.

Nine jackfruit! Not even me

Can finish nine, but let me see,

I don't suppose that they will miss one.

That was hard, but now me done.

Ten banana, mek them stay,

I feeling really full today.

M

ek me lie down on me bed, quick.

Lawd, ah feeling really sick.

Some words you may not know:

A **guinep** is a small fruit which can be popped into your mouth once you have cracked open the outer shell.

A **jackfruit** is a large, oval fruit. Inside the spiky green skin there are cream-coloured, chewy pods each containing a cream-coloured seed.

A **jew-plum** is the size of a small pear. It has sweet tangy flesh over a spiky stone.

A **naseberry** is brown and the size of a large egg. It has very sweet brown flesh and dark brown seeds.

The **red apples** in the text are Caribbean Otaheiti apples. They are pear shaped and very sweet and juicy.

Smaddy means "somebody".

A **sweet-sop** is a very sweet fruit, which has a rough outside and a white inside with black stones.